The Prin...he Pea

illustrated by **Jess Stockham**

Child's Play (International) Ltd
Ashworth Rd, Bridgemead, Swindon, SN5 7YD, UK
Swindon　　　　　　Auburn ME　　　　　　Sydney
ISBN 978-1-84643-326-9　　WP240519FUFT08193269
© 2009 Child's Play (International) Ltd
Printed in Guangdong, China
5 7 9 10 8 6
www.childs-play.com

Prince Peter was lonely.
He longed for a proper friend.
"Then find one!" advised the queen.
"Why don't you see if you can
find a nice princess?"

ADDRESS BOOK

"Good idea!" the prince replied, and off he rode.

He journeyed far and wide, looking for the perfect friend. He soon realised that it would be more difficult than he had thought.

One princess he met was interested only
in her pets, and had no time for anything else.
She smelt like all of them put together!
"Would you like to hold my dragon?" she asked.
"It won't bite you!"

Another one just wanted to do dangerous things.
"Let's go climbing first," she suggested.
"And then we'll go canoeing!"

Another one wanted to be a magician. She tried out all her meanest spells on the poor prince!

Another loved the strangest food. "Try this!" she offered. "Strawberry and Onion Pavlova!"

And one princess refused to meet him at all.

Finally, the prince returned home, sad that he had not been able to find his perfect friend.

One evening, there was a terrible storm that went on all night. The wind howled, the thunder crashed and rain swept against the windows.

Above the storm, they heard a furious knocking at the palace door. The king rushed to open it, to find a slight figure, wrapped in a dripping cloak.

"Come in, whoever you are," the king said. "Nobody should be out in this weather."

The figure came in, and took off her cloak.

"I'm Princess Petra," she explained. "Lovely palace! It's just like home. I'd love a bath!"

"Are you dry now?" asked Prince Peter. "And warm enough? Would you like something to eat? You'll stay over, of course?"

"Do you think she really is a princess?" whispered the king to the queen. "How can we tell?"

"Watch me!" replied the queen. "I know just the trick!"

The queen went to the kitchen, and asked the cook for a single pea. She went straight to the guest room to check that it was ready. She took off all the bedclothes, and put the pea on the bedstead.

Next, she put seven mattresses, one after another, on top of the pea. And on top of the mattresses she placed seven feather beds.

"Nobody will be able to feel the pea in the bed," she explained to the king, "unless they are of the finest and most royal blood."

"I'm so tired," Princess Petra yawned.
"I feel I could sleep for weeks!"

"I hope you sleep well," said the prince.
"Will you be warm enough?
Can I get you anything?"

"Just a ladder, please,"
asked the princess.
"Good night!"

But no matter how tired she was,
the princess could not sleep.

She tried lying on her back, but that did not work.
She tried counting sheep, and singing lullabies.

She tried lying on her side, with no success.

But she could not sleep, not even a single wink.

The next morning, the queen asked Princess Petra how she had slept.

"I'm afraid to say I had a terrible night," explained the princess. "Something must have kept me awake. And I've got bruises all over. What on earth can have caused them?"

"So she's definitely a princess?" whispered the king.

"No doubt of it," replied the queen. "Even I could barely feel the pea through all those mattresses. She's almost as delicate as me!"

"You poor thing," said Prince Peter.
"Those bruises look terrible, and you must
be exhausted. How can I cheer you up?
Would you like a tour of the palace?"

The prince and princess spent all day together, and discovered that they liked each other's company.

So Princess Petra stayed another day, and another, and yet another! Luckily for her, the queen removed the pea from her bed, so she had no trouble sleeping soundly for the rest of her visit!